DARKSIDE SEATTLE: MEAT

Published by Clockwork Dragon Books
clockworkdragon.net

First printing, January 2020

Darkside Seattle: Meat is a work of fiction sited in a fictional version of Seattle, WA. People, places, and incidents are either products of the author's mind or used fictitiously. No endorsement of any kind should be inferred by existing locations or organizations used within it.

No babies were harmed in the making of this book. Much cheesecake was consumed for research purposes.

ISBN: 978-1-944334-53-6

DARKSIDE SEATTLE:
MEAT

L.E. FRENCH

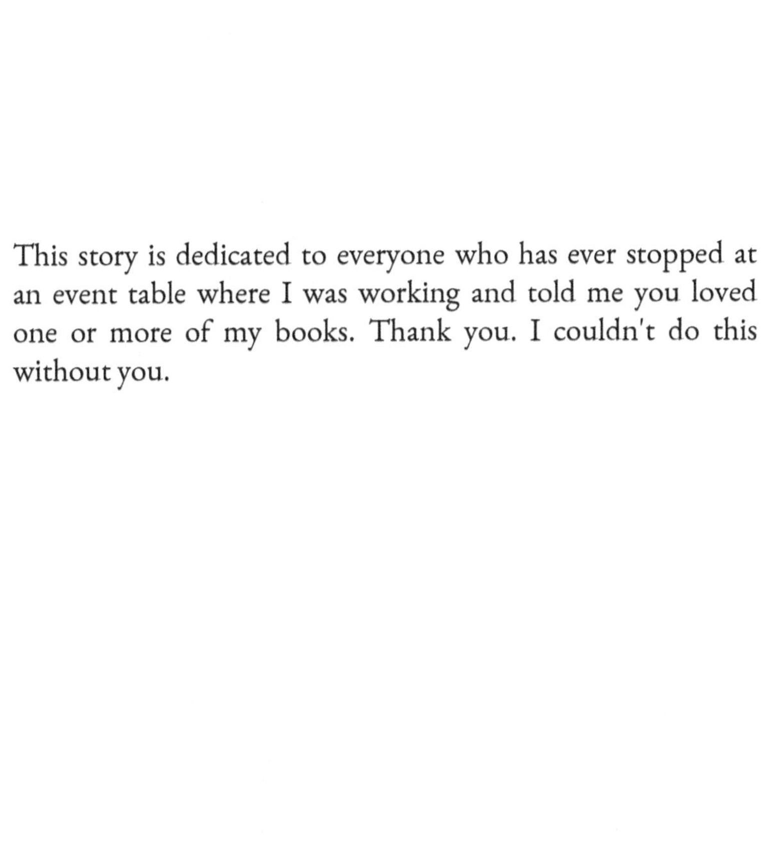

This story is dedicated to everyone who has ever stopped at an event table where I was working and told me you loved one or more of my books. Thank you. I couldn't do this without you.

CHAPTER 1

I couldn't stop re-reading the message from Godhand International. Green letters overlaid my field of vision, provided by my government-mandated cranial implant.

Thank you for your ten years of service, now go fuck off.

One moment had changed my life forever. I thought I'd done the right thing by convincing a woman not to shoot a man. Ms. Godhand had gone to jail and Mr. Lynch had taken over the company. And I'd lost my job.

Rain pattered on my regulation-cut short hair and trickled down my bare neck. A green notification flashed in my vision to alert me to the impending arrival of the light rail train that would take me home. Stepping in front of it struck me as a reasonable idea. Pun intended.

Forty minutes after I boarded the train, my wife would ask me why my paycheck hadn't cleared yet. Two weeks ago, security had marched me out of the building. Godhand HR hadn't sent the firing notice until I'd reached the lobby.

I hadn't told Lisa yet. She thought I kept reporting at work. Instead, I'd spent all this time trying to find another job.

Every single person I talked to had seen my face on the news. They'd all turned me down flat. Lisa considered me a hero. The rest of the world considered me untouchable.

"Do I know you?" The speaker, a man in a trench coat with polished black shoes, squinted at me. He looked like every other twenty-something suit prowling Seattle. At least he hadn't jumped into a vat of cheap cologne before leaving his home.

"I don't think so."

"Oh, I know." He snapped his fingers. "You fucked your career on video by revealing your loyalty to Victoria over Ross."

I scowled. "Thanks for the remi— Wait. How did you know about my job?"

He grinned and pointed up the street. "Walk with me, Dave."

This asshole knew me, which meant he'd targeted me. Two things could happen if I joined him. One, he'd lure me into an ambush. Two, he'd lure me into an ambush.

I could handle myself against one guy. My gut said this asshole brought friends.

"Fuck off." I hunched my shoulders and turned toward the oncoming train. Taking my chances with Lisa seemed better than dealing with this fucker. Lisa had promised to love me for better or worse.

"I have a job for you."

I threw him my best annoyed glare. "No one has a job for me."

"Then call me No One." He offered me a card.

The shiny white train arrived. People pushed through the doors. I took the damned card and stepped into the car. The train pinged my implant and flashed me a welcome message with a reminder that my monthly ride pass expired in one week. Did I want to renew now? No. I indicated my desired station and it left me alone.

Why did I take the card? I didn't know. To make that

guy go away, I supposed. I stuffed it into my jacket pocket. Finding no open seats, I stood and held the plastic railing two inches over my head

Lisa would understand. I'd tried my best to keep this disaster from hitting her. She'd appreciate that. We had a three-month-old baby, so everything would suck for the foreseeable future, but she'd understand. She might even help me find something else I was qualified to do.

The train snaked through the city on magnetic rails, smooth and silent. A canned female voice announced the stations. People in the car stared forward like empty zombies, ignoring the view of overhead traffic through the glass-top canopy. Most probably read essays and articles or messaged others through their implants. Sweat and deodorant mingled with cologne and perfume in a messy, human stench I'd gotten used to a long time ago.

Halfway home, curiosity and boredom nudged me enough to pull out the card and check it. One side had a 'link code and the name "Jay Smith." So original. The other side was blank.

What if Jay Smith had a real job for me? He'd stalked me enough to know where to find me, and he knew I hadn't landed another job yet. What kind of guy wanted to hire someone when no one else did?

Whatever Jay Smith wanted me to do, I had a feeling I didn't want to do it. Lisa and I would talk. Things would turn out fine. We'd make it work.

Convinced I could manage this, I stuck the card in my pocket again. I didn't need charity from some freak with a fake name.

When the train reached my station, my implant pinged me a reminder to get out. I shuffled off with a dozen other people and headed up a plascrete pedestrian alley between towering apartment buildings with a wide variety of shops catering to my income bracket on the ground floor.

The rain had stopped for the moment, leaving a brisk, gritty wind blowing in my face. Black, brown, yellow, and green mold clung to the walls. Grassy weeds as tall as my waist grew from cracks.

Kids passed through often to pluck anything edible from those patches of life. Dandelion leaves tasted better than the fake, soy-based shit we all ate down here.

At least no one in my neighborhood had to stoop to eating Processed Food Product, otherwise known as shit-in-a-can. We all retained that much dignity.

My building had pathetic security, but it stood out in the area. Our fifteenth-floor apartment offered the best we could afford near a light rail line. Without that, we would've had to buy cars. Even a shitty old internal combustion car cost too much for us.

I approached the front door with its plastic plants and plassteel bars. The building's system pinged my implant and buzzed the door open for me. Like it had every day for ten years, the stale, empty smell of the bleach-heavy lobby greeted me.

People I'd seen every day for years passed me on their way in or out. We acknowledged each other with brief moments of eye contact and slight nods.

As soon as I stood inside the faux wood elevator with its industrial, vomit-colored carpet and light notes of urine and cat, reality hit me like a ton of bricks. I'd reached the point when I couldn't lie to Lisa anymore. She took care of our finances. I opened jars and reached things on high shelves.

Since she hadn't messaged me to ask about it yet, I figured she hadn't checked our account yet.

Our hallway had more terrible carpet. Cheap plastic

housings covered little yellow lights on the popcorn ceiling. Fake wood doors with plastic numbers interrupted the bland beige walls. Everything smelled like wet dog despite the fact no one on our floor owned one.

Someone else walked up the hallway. Absorbed in my thoughts, I noted nothing more than a familiar face and nodded to them.

Number twelve accepted my ID and opened the door for me. I walked into our tiny kitchen and stepped out of my shoes to leave them beside Lisa's. My jacket went on a hook above them, also beside Lisa's. Nothing separated the kitchen from the living area with its couch and video display.

Beyond it, a glass door opened on our balcony. The enclosed concrete space had enough room for two plastic patio chairs and a single planter with three fading strawberry plants. They'd served us well this year, providing a few berries every day through May, June, and July.

The most beautiful woman I'd ever seen in my life emerged from the short hallway leading to our bedroom and bathroom in sweatpants and a nursing bra, carrying our son, Aaron. She wore her dark hair in a thick ponytail with stray hairs floating loose around her head. My son made no noise, and my wife looked less tired than she had for the past three months.

"How was your day, dear?" She yawned in the middle of the question.

How could I tell her bad news at a time like this? "Same as always. How about yours?" Baby weight still clung to her hips and belly, but I didn't care. The sight of her always made me smile.

"We went to the park." She sighed. "I got a notice from work. If I don't go back in the next two weeks, they're going to hire on the temp they have covering my job and fire me."

Fuck.

"So I spent most of another day trying to find a daycare option that won't blow a hole in our budget," she grumbled. "I swear, it's like they think people who have babies suddenly become rich because of it."

Double fuck.

"I don't know what to do." Lisa turned her back on me, swishing her hips to rock Aaron.

If she lost her job over this, they'd probably demand we pay back her maternity benefits. That would sink us so deep into debt we'd be lucky to eat shit-in-a-can for the rest of our lives. Especially if I couldn't find another job.

"I got fired," my mouth blurted. The words spun into the world, out of my control, as if I somehow thought they would help the situation.

My pulse sped, my mouth dried, and my eyes watered.

Lisa turned and blinked at me. She opened her mouth and shut it, then she squinted at me. "What?"

She didn't think she'd heard me right. If I wanted, I could twist the words into something else. I could play with it all and make it a joke.

No, dammit. I said it. We had to figure things out. I'd come home expecting to tell her, and my cowardly ass didn't get to back out like this.

I gulped. "They fired me. For talking down Ms. Godhand instead of shooting her. The media called me a hero and the new boss called me a traitor." Saying it out loud hurt me in ways I couldn't explain.

Her fine, delicate brow furrowed. "When?"

"Two days after it happened." All kinds of reactions played in my head. As soon as she wrapped her head around it, she'd get upset and want to know why I'd lied to her. Time to head off that shit. "I've been trying like crazy to get a new job so we wouldn't miss more than one paycheck. I didn't want you to worry, which was dumb, but I can't find anything. No one will hire me. I've been blackballed. Except this one guy who gave me his card." I held up Jay Smith's card.

Why did I bring up Mr. Smith? He seemed dodgy as fuck, and I didn't want Lisa tangled in anything like that.

Her lovely, delicate fingers plucked the card from my hand. She frowned at it. "I don't understand." Everything about her body language flashed warning signs at me. One wrong nudge and she'd flash into anger.

"Neither do I." Torn between clinging to her and slumping in failure, I rubbed my face. At least now she knew. The weight of pretending for her, of acting content when I wanted to scream, sloughed off my shoulders. A different kind of weight took its place. "He stopped me on the street after yet another rejection. Knew my name, knew all about me."

She nodded and studied the back of the card as if it had information only for her. The way she turned her back on me again made me panic.

"I'm sorry I lied to you."

"Of course you are." She sounded distant.

I'd fucked myself. Hard. "I should've told you right away. I thought I could find another job fast enough it wouldn't matter. They just keep turning me down. I don't even think I can get work as a barista right now."

"Mmhmmm."

I had a feeling I'd be lucky if she let me sleep on the couch for a while.

Lisa held out the card to give it back. "Mr. Smith will meet you in an hour at the old sports complex."

I blinked at her. "What?"

"He has a short-term job for you. It pays. If you handle it well, he'll have something longer term." She shooed me toward the door. "Go."

My wife had taken the card for Jay Smith, contacted him, and set up an interview for me. The moment felt absurd. "That's in the Darkside. It's probably illegal."

"Dave. You just told me you can't get work." Lisa pointed at the card. Anger burbled in her tone. "This man wants to hire you. We have a baby, and my boss wants to fire me for it, so you get your ass out that door and you go talk to him."

Her anger reared its head and poised like a cobra to strike.

"Yes, dear." I slipped on my shoes and scuttled out the damned door because I'm not fucking stupid.

Whatever happened at the old stadium, I doubted it would keep me from having to sleep on the couch.

CHAPTER 2

The closest light rail station still forced me to walk two miles to reach the location. I kept my hands in my pockets and my head down as I hurried to make my appointment.

[DavidMartinSystem: WAINet signal is weak in this area. Some services may not be available.]

On one side of the street, the buildings had iron bars over the windows, fresh paint, and signs of regular maintenance.

On the other side, chunks of concrete bigger than me littered the ground around the stadium. They'd fallen a long time ago and no one had ever removed them. Each probably still had corpses under them.

At least I reached the place in daylight. They didn't call it Darkside for no reason.

Even cops didn't go into the Darkside. But here I was, rushing into the forsaken land like an idiot to meet my destiny or some shit like that.

Jay Smith leaned against a black sedan, still looking like an asshole in a suit. He raised a hand to greet me with a smug-ass grin.

I crossed a street with a gaping hole twenty feet to my left and a chunk of concrete the size of a tow truck fifty feet to my right. No need to worry about traffic, at least.

"Glad you made it," Jay said as I reached him.

Though I wanted to tell him to fuck off, I grunted.

"Your wife seems nice."

"What's the job?" I growled.

He grinned more, the asshole. "A tryout. I've got someone who needs a lookout for a few hours. You'll never meet them, so there's no liability." Jay opened his car door and gestured for me to get into the passenger seat. "I'll drop you off so you don't have to walk."

I peered into the car, expecting someone with a knife in the back seat, waiting to slit my throat. The fucking thing had the gall to smell like new leather. "Why should I trust you?"

He shrugged. "I work for Victoria. She rewards loyalty."

That didn't explain anything. "Ms. Godhand is in jail."

"A true statement." Jay gestured to the open car door again. "Get in, Dave. I'm here to rescue you from the gutter. You're not going to get a better offer anytime soon."

Lisa's anger flashed in my head.

I got into the car.

Jay circled to the driver's side and slid in beside me. We shut the doors. The car lifted off the ground. Unlike normal people, Jay used a steering wheel, foot pedals, and altitude control lever to drive the thing.

"Your job is easy, I just need someone I can trust not to walk away in the middle. You stand where I tell you for six hours and keep watch. Unless you see someone you think doesn't belong, every thirty minutes, you text an all-clear to a 'link code I'll give you. If you do see someone questionable, you text a description of that person to that 'link code right away. If you get any instructions from that 'link code, you follow them. That's it."

I sat with my arms crossed over my chest, more uncomfortable than words could express. Every word out of this guy's mouth rubbed me wrong. "You want me to be a security guard for a short night shift?"

"Yes, exactly."

"Why?"

"Since this is your first time out, I'll let that question slide. Never ask me again. 'Why' is above your pay grade. You need to know what to do and where to do it. That is the sum total of the information at your disposal. Rest secure in the knowledge that it isn't my intention to fuck you over or get you killed. That would be counterproductive."

His intentions meant jack-fucking-squat to me. "You came to me," I snapped. "If you don't want to tell me, then set the car down and let me the fuck out."

Jay raised an eyebrow and glanced at me. "I'll pay you two weeks' salary to do it, and I'll transfer it when you finish the job."

That shut me right the fuck up. I needed that money to make rent on time, and he wanted to give it to me for six hours of work. If I let slip to Lisa that I'd given up that much money over something stupid like scruples, she'd throw me out for the night.

"Fine," I said, glaring out the side window. "Do I get a gun or anything?"

"No. Just rent money and the possibility of more work in the future. As a value-added bonus, this is all under the table, which means no taxes get deducted."

Sure. No strings attached, just a noose dragging me deeper into this shit.

"Great. Anything else I get to know about this job?"

"I'll pick you up where I drop you off. You'll get a notice when you're clear to leave, which might happen early. If it does, that won't affect your pay. Oh, and you keep your mouth shut. Don't even tell your wife the details. She doesn't need to know where you were or what you did. No one does."

I couldn't think of another question to ask, so I shrugged.

Jay lowered the car into an area full of buildings between ten and fifteen floors tall. The intact street had one lane for local traffic and one lane for parking in both directions. All the structures had signs proclaiming the companies using them as office space, which explained the notable lack of cars skimming the road or pedestrians on the sidewalk at this hour.

Regular people with office jobs didn't work this late. At Godhand International, the offices mostly cleared by six in the evening and stayed vacant all weekend. Only the big bosses came and went at weird hours. I'd worked every security shift during my time there, so I knew the routines.

He pulled a card out of his pocket and handed it to me. "This is the 'link code. You have six minutes to reach that building, which should be plenty of time." He pointed out the front windshield at a glassy building two blocks up, on the other side of the street. "Loiter near the front doors. That's your post. Check in when you get there."

Though I didn't want to do any of this, I took the card and got out of the car. I needed the money. If I repeated that to myself enough times, maybe I could get through this.

Taking a brisk walking pace, I headed for the building. Green-tinted glass covered all the building's dozen or so floors. The front wall of glass offered a view of the dimly-lit, tastefully decorated lobby.

No one sat at the front desk, suggesting either a single guard making rounds or a fully automated system. I scanned the alcove shielding the front door from the weather and didn't see any cameras.

That, of course, meant they'd spent money on camouflaging them.

The building's AR system pinged my implant. I had the option to allow it to provide an overlay on my vision, which I declined. Seeing their fancy Augmented Reality shit instead of the actual street wouldn't improve my night.

[CarrierHoldingsSystem: Welcome to Carrier Holdings. Our regular business hours are 8am to 6pm. Outside these hours, our lobby is closed.]

Thank you, Carrier Holdings. The company name sounded familiar, but I couldn't think why. Maybe I'd seen it in the news for some reason or they owned my apartment building.

Not that it mattered. All these fucking corporations did all the same shitty crap. They were basically interchangeable.

I sent a check-in to the 'link code on the card, then tucked it back into my pocket.

[JSModule: DavidMartin is checked in at 19:43, two minutes early.]

Lucky me, I got to spend an extra two minutes at this place, going above and beyond expectations.

My implant account automatically created an address book entry for JSModule, like it did every time I messaged a new account. CarrierHoldingsSystem didn't get to create an address book entry for me unless I interacted with it. Automatic messages couldn't do that.

Corporations could access implant registries, of course, but they couldn't log my presence unless I said something.

At least, that was what the government told us. I had my doubts. A lot of people did.

Interestingly, though, JSModule's message disappeared as soon as I closed it. Every other message I'd ever received, I could view anytime. Even those I deleted still lived on a server someplace. If I knew what to search for, I could pull up deleted messages.

Not so for JSModule's message. It evaporated as if it'd never existed.

How did Jay do that? I doubted he'd tell me.

After scanning the street and the lobby once, I picked a spot near the front door and leaned against the glass wall. I had no idea how to look casual anymore, so I didn't bother trying. If a cop skimmed past, I'd act like I'd stopped where the weather couldn't affect me to read an article through my implant. People did that.

About five minutes after I checked in, Jay's car lifted off. He'd stayed long enough to watch me take up a position and get comfortable. Yes, Mr. Smith, I would do the job as ordered and not screw off.

Once he left, the street was empty. The exhaust of hovercar fuel drifted on the air. Time plodded past. I'd spent ten years doing this exact job, except inside a building instead of outside one. Boredom didn't bother me. All the usual instincts took over, keeping me alert.

Ten minutes later, the Carrier Holdings automated message hit me again.

Movement caught my eye inside the lobby. A cleaning bot, this one a three-foot cube on rollers with brushes, emerged from a sliding door in the wall and set to work buffing the floor. I watched it for half a minute to make sure no one sprang out of it and nothing else unexpected happened.

The cleaning bot did its job. I ignored it and continued to do mine.

My first check-in passed with nothing to report. The sun set behind the clouds, and I kept watching. Streetlights on iron posts flickered on. I moved to a shadow cast by my target building's overhang.

Two check-ins later, a nondescript black sedan hovercar skimmed down the other side of the street, going way under the speed limit.

I pinged the car for its plate number. Anyone could do that. Only cops could get additional information. And, I assumed, people like Jay.

Once my system reported back, I sent a message with a description and plate number to the 'link code.

Five minutes passed. The same car or one exactly like it hovered up my side of the street. It stopped at the curb in front of me. I watched the window whirr down. A guy stuck his head out with a dopey, drunk-ass grin and beckoned for me to come closer.

"Hey," he slurred. "Gimme a hand."

Something about him didn't seem right to me. What kind of drunk idiot skimmed down a road like this at nine-thirty at night? A big boss, maybe, but no one else. This guy had the wrong look, though. Corporate execs didn't let their hair grow out that much, they didn't wear ties that cheap, and they sure as fuck didn't wave down random strangers on the street.

People at that level had servants to wipe their asses.

I composed a description and sent it to the 'link code as I approached. "I'm trying to read, asshole. What the fuck do you want?" Wary of a trap, I stopped far enough away that he couldn't reach out and snag any part of me without moving so much that I'd have time to react.

"Hey, man, relax." The guy waved a white sheet of paper with a bunch of bumps stuck to it in neat lines of different colors. Each bump was the size of my pinky fingernail. Party drugs came like that, or so I'd seen on the news. "The screen between the front and back of the car is broken. Pass this to the bitches in back."

The fuck?

"Take a hit if you want."

He sounded way too coherent for the amount of slurring he used. Everything I'd ever learned flashed warning signs in my head.

I wished I had a gun.

"Get out and do it yourself, asshole." I backed away from the car, half-expecting him to shoot me.

"Fuck you," the guy growled.

The car shot up the street, then banked into the air.

As soon as I lost sight of him, my whole body shook with reaction. Years ago, an interaction like that wouldn't have bothered me much. I'd gotten soft from cushy postings.

I leaned against my slice of wall, ignored the Carrier Holdings automated message, and wished like hell that I could afford body armor.

CHAPTER 3

I shook my shit back into shape and did the rest of my shift. Nothing else happened. Ten minutes before my last check-in, JSModule sent me an all-clear to leave my post and call the job done. Jay's nondescript black sedan arrived at the pickup point five seconds before I did.

When I slid into the passenger seat, Jay flashed me a grin.

"Nice work." He tossed a small tube at me.

I bobbled the thing, dropped it onto the floor, and had to pat around my feet to pick it up. Holding it up, I had no idea what to make of it. The tube had a port of some kind I'd never seen before on one end. Otherwise, it appeared to be a solid metal tube about the size of Lisa's pinky finger.

"The fuck is this?" I held it up.

Jay laughed. "You're so raw, Dave. It's cute."

"I'm glad I amuse you," I grumbled.

"That's your payment." He handed me a thin cable with a jack for the tube on one end and a weird little metal plate on the other. "That's how you access it. No charge for that. Call it a welcome gift. The plate is an induction pad for your implant. Plug it into the drive, stick the pad behind your ear, and push the pad like a button."

I had two questions. One, I kept to myself. Jay obviously

operated outside the law, so asking why he wanted to give me an induction pad counted as stupid. The second one, I asked while I followed his instructions. "Why don't they just make the drive thing with the pad attached?"

He shrugged. "The pad is illegal. The drive isn't."

Sure. Folks could get all the drives they wanted and use them some other way. I didn't have anything I could plug the cable into, but I supposed other people did. Rich people, probably.

As soon as I pushed on the pad, it activated with a tiny whine. My visual overlay pinged with a notification. The skin behind my ear itched.

[DaveMartinSystem: Registering new data unit attachment. Do you wish to access this data?]

[DaveMartin: Yes.]

I hadn't attached it for no reason, right?

[DaveMartinSystem: Accessing data.............]

"Do I need to do anything in particular?"

"Nope," Jay said. "Any of these I give you will be pre-programmed to access your account and transfer funds without leaving a tracer. Because I like you and want to employ you again, I'll point out that people with less interest in your well-being can put viruses on these things."

"Great." Nothing like setting me up as his slave.

[DaveMartinSystem: Data access complete. Account modification initiated.]

"Wait. Account modification? What's it modifying?"

"Your bank balance."

I blinked at him. "What?"

"Relax. It's real money moving from one account to another." He smirked. "Or, at least, it's digital money. Who knows if any of it's actually real anymore. Point is, we're not just changing numbers in a database, we're making an actual transfer. Just changing numbers in a database is a thousand times harder to get away with."

Not a thousand times harder to do, of course.

[DaveMartinSystem: Account modification complete. Disengage data unit attachment?]

[DaveMartin: Yes.]

The induction pad popped off my skin. I rubbed the spot it had stuck to.

"Don't touch that. You'll tear the flesh and bleed all over my car. Besides, cops notice that kind of damage and question it."

I froze my hand and pulled it away from my neck. "Thanks."

"Give me back the drive, but you can keep the cord."

"Gee, I can keep the super-illegal part? That's a great deal!" I popped out the cord and handed him the drive.

Jay snorted. "You get one more freebie from me, Dave. After this, there's always a price tag." He set down the car in front of my apartment building. "You want to bring that cable with you on every job. I won't supply you with another one for free, not even to borrow for two minutes, and you don't get to take my drives with you."

He handed me a wad of soft, black cloth small enough to fit inside his fist. "Keep it inside this."

I took the cloth and discovered it was a sleeve.

"That's a shielded bag. Scanners won't pick up the pad so long as it's inside that. They'd have to do a physical search. If you get to that point, you're already fucked. One more thing won't matter."

Fuck me and my life.

Sitting in his car with an illegal piece of equipment in one hand and a bag to protect it in the other, I wanted to laugh or scream, or maybe cry. Something. I'd just done my first illegal job and now had an illegal piece of hardware plus the means to keep it safe.

Jay shooed me out of his car. "I recommend you have a drink, fuck your wife, and get some sleep. I'll call when I have another job for you."

"Yeah." That all sounded shitty and great at the same time. "I guess I should thank you."

"You really should. Go home, Dave."

I shambled out of the car in a daze. The building recognized me and opened the door. For the first time, I noticed absolutely nothing about my surroundings as I stumbled into the elevator and pushed the twelve button out of habit.

If I wanted to, I could still walk away. The next time Jay summoned me, I could give back the cord in its bag and tell him never to contact me again.

And I'd pay the bills with...my winning personality?

No one but Jay wanted to employ me. He'd said Victoria Godhand rewarded loyalty, and I'd shown that. If I thought of these jobs as working for her, then it wouldn't seem so bad. She had a side company that paid me to do weird contract jobs.

Really, had I done anything terrible? No, not at all. I'd stood in front of a wall and done my job as a security guard. The questionable parts all surrounded the hiring and payment, not the job itself.

I could live with that.

The elevator dumped me onto my floor. I reached my door without paying attention. Inside, all the lights stayed off despite my entry. Weak starlight painted the carpet in the living room section, giving me enough light to leave my shoes by the door and not walk into a wall on the way to the bedroom.

In the kitchen, I paused forever, trying to remember if I'd finished off that bottle of shitty whiskey in the cabinet above the fridge.

Regardless of my opinions about Jay, he had some solid advice.

Shit, I had no idea. Fuck it. I put my hand on the wall and let it guide me down our short hallway to the bedroom. Our bathroom was at the other end.

Lisa had left the door open for me or I would've walked into it. She'd have the baby lying on her chest.

In the dark, I moved around the bed by rote memory. We had a narrow strip of maybe two feet between the bed and the closet. The dresser on the side had exactly enough space for the drawers to open.

Between the dresser and the door, we had our one luxury item, an instant clothes cleaner. Put dirty cloth in, wait five minutes, get clean cloth out. Saved us from needing much of a wardrobe or places to store it all. Machine made a lot of noise, though. At least, it made a lot of noise compared to the sound of Lisa and the baby sleeping.

I stripped in the dark, thinking about that guy in the car who'd asked me to pass party drugs to the back seat.

Why hadn't he pulled out a gun and shot me? Because he could have. I'd bet my balls that guy had faked drunkenness. He sure as fuck hadn't needed someone to pass anything to the back seat.

Maybe Jay had sent him to test me.

The more I considered that, the more sense it made. If he had access to Victoria Godhand's money, then he could afford to throw around a lot more than he'd paid me for a simple test to see if he could trust a guy.

Jay Smith needed people who wouldn't squeal on him, but he also needed people who could do the fucking job.

That guy had scared the shit out of me. I wondered what else he did for Jay.

At some point, I'd probably find out. Assuming I lived that long.

Fuck me, I needed to pick up some life insurance or something. Godhand International had provided us with a sizable amount, along with my health care and discounts at the company store.

We'd lost a hell of a lot more than just my salary. When Lisa's boss fired her for having a baby, we'd get fucked hard.

Of course, the job I'd just done wouldn't have interfered with me taking care of the kid during the day. In fact, if Jay had me do stuff mostly at night, I could watch the baby while Lisa went to work every day.

Huh.

I'd learned how during my generous GI paternity leave of eight weeks.

This whole thing might turn out okay.

Without bothering to find pajamas, I climbed into bed and slid next to Lisa. As expected, she lay on her back with the baby on her chest. I patted them gently until I touched the soft fuzz on Aaron's head.

Between this kid and Jay Smith, I had a whole lot of hope for the future.

I sent a command to the apartment system to give me a hint of light in the bedroom. Just enough to see the two things that mattered in my life.

The system brought up the lights with a soft orangey glow, like the moments before sunrise when the day still had potential not to turn to shit. Aaron slept in a cute little sack with only his head and tiny hands bare. His tiny head, lying on Lisa's chest, faced me.

Even in sleep, Lisa cradled the baby with both hands.

She wore a nursing bra and sweatpants, as she'd done since Aaron was born. Her brown hair splayed across her pillow.

Their calm and peace put me to sleep. The baby's hungry cries woke me when I needed to get up and pretend to go to work.

Except I didn't need to pretend anymore.

Tension bled from my body while Lisa sat up to change the baby's diaper. She did that on the dresser.

"I have a plan," I said.

"Oh?" She worked fast, with swift, sure hands.

I could handle a diaper change but she did it better than me. Mommy magic.

"Jay wants me to do stuff at night. You work during the day."

She finished with the baby and brought him back to bed to feed him. Lying on her side with her back to me, she performed more mommy magic out of my sight.

Eager to touch her, I scooted behind her and spooned her body. She cushioned her head on my arm and I wrapped the other one around her waist. The baby had forced me to give up her breasts, but nothing else.

"I accept your plan," Lisa said.

Thank fuck. I ran my hand down her thigh and kissed her neck. "Set him aside when you're done?"

"Did you get paid for last night?"

"He paid me right away."

"How much?"

Hoping to distract her, I slipped my hand between her legs. "Exactly what he promised. Rent is covered. We're fine. I'll work for him at night when he calls, and you can keep your job so we have the regular income."

She turned her head enough to kiss me. "Good job. I'll get excited when he calls you a second time."

"I'd like you to get excited right now."

With a snort, she rolled her eyes at me. "Your dick can wait until Aaron is done."

"Yes, dear."

CHAPTER 4

The next morning, Lisa told her boss she'd found a babysitter and would return to work in a week. She had to get used to pumping breastmilk and I had to get used to dealing with it. We spent that time trying to settle into the groove with Aaron.

I heard nothing from Jay for the entire week. Despite everything he'd said and the cord he'd gifted me, I couldn't help but wonder if he really meant he wanted me to work for him.

[JaySmith: I have something for you. Tomorrow, noon.]

Lisa had taken Aaron for a walk, so she didn't hear me growl under my breath as I dried the dishes.

Good thing I'd spent six days working on shifting my sleep schedule to stay up late for Jay's night jobs. Asshole.

[DaveMartin: Find someone else. I have a baby to watch.]

[JaySmith: That's funny because your wife said the same thing. I've arranged for a babysitter to take your kid while you handle this.]

He'd messaged Lisa first? What the fuck?

I put away the last plate from lunch and glared at the wall.

[DaveMartin: I thought you said not to tell my wife

anything.]

[JaySmith: That's true. I did. And I meant it. But in this case, she's involved. You're going to meet her at work for a surprise lunch date. The rest you'll get when you check in.]

[DaveMartin: You're hiring me to take my wife to lunch?]

[JaySmith: Yep. Bring the kid. Your babysitter will meet you after you check in at 3rd and Battery.]

[DaveMartin: That's Lisa's workplace.]

[JaySmith: Those keen observation skills are half the reason I like you, Dave. Good luck.]

What. The fuck.

I stared at the wall, trying to make sense of any of this.

Lisa opened the door to return before I managed to figure out how to word a text about this. She breezed past me, headed for the bathroom or bedroom.

"I ran into Jay." She made it sound like Jay was an old school pal she had coffee with once in a while.

That fucker hadn't messaged Lisa first, he'd walked up and talked to her. After telling me to keep her out of everything, he'd strolled up and introduced himself.

Worse, he'd done it when she had the baby.

"Oh really?" Trying to sound casual, I followed her from several paces behind and stopped in the bedroom doorway to watch her change Aaron's diaper. "How's he doing?"

She snorted. "He wants me to get something from my job for him."

"And you said yes?" The woman I married wouldn't have done that. At least, I didn't think so.

The woman I married liked to have sex with me, though, and we hadn't done that in months. Maybe I didn't know her as well as I thought.

"He said he could hire a team to do it, but he'd rather have a higher chance of success and give us the money instead." She moved with swift purpose, wiping the baby's butt and replacing the diaper mechanically.

The money problem had affected her as much as me. It turned off judgment for both of us.

Not that I'd say so to Lisa. "You're okay with the babysitter part?"

She cleared off the used diaper and scooped up Aaron. Facing me, she glared with a dare for me to argue or try to back out. "Yes. He made promises and I believe him. We'll have lunch, I'll pass you a data chip, and then he'll pay us a lot of money."

A data chip? Lisa worked as a secretary for an architectural firm. What the fuck did Jay want from an architectural firm?

Not that he'd tell me. Above my pay grade.

"And you're okay with the rest of it? Stealing from your boss..."

With a dismissive wave, she sat on the bed and whipped out a breast to feed Aaron. "It's not a big deal."

Not a big deal? Who was this woman? "But—"

"I said it's not a big deal." Her voice carried a hint of a growl.

"Yes, dear." I left the room and dropped onto the couch. Working for Jay wasn't supposed to involve Lisa.

What next? Smuggling data chips in Aaron's diaper?

Fuck me, I would not ever say that out loud. If Jay thought for one moment I would accept that, he'd ask for it.

I covered my face and tried not to think about all the ways this could go wrong.

In my head, I saw Lisa at her desk, calling up files and transferring them to a data chip. In the middle, her boss walks up and asks what she's doing. The cops arrive because he's already called them. They arrest her. My son's mother, the only woman I'd ever wanted for more than a day, goes to jail forever.

Fuck. Maybe there had never been a choice. Once Jay snared me, he'd snared my whole family whether I liked it or not.

Lisa pushed my shoulders back and sat on my lap. She'd left her shirt behind to tease me with her nursing bra. "It'll be fine. You worry too much."

"Sure." I set my hands on her waist and stared at her chest without seeing anything except disaster on the horizon. "What does he even want?"

"Some old building plans."

Though I wanted to ask why, I knew Jay hadn't told her. As he'd done with me, he would've quoted a payment high enough to make her stop asking questions.

"We need the money," Lisa said.

Yes, we did. Without the baby, I thought we could've scraped by until I managed to find something else.

Aaron had changed all the math for us.

For a brief moment, I hated him for that.

I sighed. "I just don't like you doing things for him. It's not safe. You should be able to go to your job and not worry about getting caught doing illegal things."

"So should you." She raked her fingers through my hair and forced me to lean back until my head rested against the wall.

"Maybe I should come down to your work early. I can act like a lookout while you handle the files. You pretend you just have to finish this one thing before you go."

She smirked and kissed me, erasing all my thoughts. I slipped my hands over her smooth, soft skin. Her hips rocked over mine.

I missed this.

Aaron cried.

Lisa broke off the kiss and abandoned me without a word.

That little shit. He knew. Somehow, he knew and decided to stop us.

I scooted to the edge of the couch and rubbed my face. Lisa's voice drifted in the air as she soothed the baby. She brought him with her when she returned.

Sometimes, I really hated being a dad.

Eventually, we'd have to find a way to afford a two-bedroom place or I'd never get laid again. I could see those nightmare moments with Aaron interrupting us on the horizon. Instead of crying, he'd ask why Mommy is naked and groaning.

Assuming we ever fucked again, of course.

"We'll pick this up later," Lisa said.

Sure. Later. She meant tomorrow or next week, not later tonight. I knew that because she needed the sleep. Her job demanded focus and would probably exhaust her for the first week back.

I nodded and adjusted my pants. At least my erection had already started to fade. Nothing like the wail of a baby to put a lid on that.

We moved through the rest of the day avoiding skin contact and barely speaking. I made dinner. She took Aaron to bed while I stayed up.

The next morning, when she passed the baby to me, I kissed her cheek and said goodbye. I sat on the couch with him. My mind wandered nowhere. We watched some news and a dumb movie.

Eventually, I showered, shaved, and put on my suit.

Aaron's diaper bag held three thousand things, including actual diapers. I thought I looked weird carrying it.

Something about a bag plastered with ducklings and bunnies didn't sit right with the security guard still inside me. The bright colors stood out too much. It made me a target instead of letting me fade into the background.

A baby on my arm didn't help.

We left with plenty of time to reach Lisa's work.

As soon as I stepped onto the next light rail car, it pinged my implant with a notice that my most recent monthly pass expired in four more hours. Yes, I wanted to renew it this time.

Maybe I needed my own transportation. Somehow, I had to get to places and save for a hoverbike at the same time. If Jay didn't pay me more than my job had, I'd never manage it. My income had covered rent and utilities. I still needed to do that.

Lisa couldn't pick up the slack for long. Not with a baby. We'd starve.

The mere idea of having the ability to save money for once taunted me.

No, dipshit. Focus. Never count money before you have it.

The train flashed across the city. Total cloud cover promised rain soon, like it did most of the time. Aaron gurgled and gaped at everything. As far as I knew, he'd never ridden the light rail before.

Props to him for not freaking out or screeching during the ride.

I had to switch at Pike Station to a smaller tram. As usual during the day, tourists thronged the station. People stood aside for me and smiled at Aaron.

Maybe I needed to travel with the baby more often.

Sure, if I wanted everyone to notice me all the time.

The nearly-empty tram, gleaming white and smelling of humanity, had space for about twenty people, less than half the size of a light rail car. Three other people rode it with Aaron and me. I noticed them because they all watched us.

Then I noticed the one guy because he had been the asshole driver of that car on my first mission. He wore a hat with his jeans and t-shirt and had different hair, but I recognized him anyway.

Beside me, a dusky-skinned woman wore business casual with walking shoes and a matching purse. She had a bit of a belly bump and clearly only cared about wanting to amuse Aaron. Her active interest in the baby caught my interest, hardcore.

The other man had the glazed-zombie look of a person using his implant. He probably only stared in my direction because his seat faced mine.

If Jay wanted the one guy to work with me, I thought someone would say so.

On the other hand, maybe Jay wanted to check if I'd notice the guy.

Fuck, I had no idea.

I practiced my ability to watch someone without watching them, which I did a thousand times better than that asshole.

The woman seemed much more harmless anyway, so I paid a lot more attention to her. Someone who acted innocent had a lot more potential to catch a person off-guard.

At my stop, the zombie stayed in his seat. Both the asshole and the woman stood. I decided I preferred not to exit with both of them. Walking from the next stop, especially when I still had plenty of time, wouldn't cause me any serious problems.

The woman turned and waved at Aaron with a cute little smile as the doors shut. One step ahead of her, the asshole stuck his hands in his pockets and walked.

"Weirdos everywhere," I murmured to Aaron as the tram left the stop.

"No shit," the zombie said. "I thought they'd never get off the fucking tram." He pointed a gun at me.

Ah, fuck.

CHAPTER 5

First, I wanted that gun. Second, I had no idea why anyone would point a gun at me. Third, shit, someone held a gun pointed at me.

The guy had my full and complete attention. I noticed he wore ordinary jeans, unremarkable sneakers suitable for running up wet streets, and a grey hooded sweatshirt. Everything about him politely asked for anyone nearby to ignore him as part of the background.

Like I'd done.

"Hi," I said. Somehow, I avoided sounding like a person with a gun pointed at him. Just two normal dudes in a tram, having a private chat. No big deal. "I think you've got the wrong guy."

He grinned. "David Martin? Person responsible for Victoria Godhand walking away alive?"

His word choice said a lot about his intent.

Fuck.

Desperate not to let him see my terror, I focused on Aaron. Babies made great distractions.

I shot a quick message to JSModule. Maybe Jay could get that asshole back on the tram before anything bad happened.

[DavidMartin: Delayed by gunman on tram.]

"I'm going to take your shocked silence as confirmation," the guy said.

The seats on the tram probably wouldn't stop bullets.

I cleared my throat and hoped the guy wanted to threaten me instead of kill me. "I don't know that I'd say she 'walked away.' "

[JSModule: What's he want?]

How interesting that Jay could drop into the JSModule and use it to send and receive non-recorded messages.

He laughed. "Okay, that's fair. But still, she's alive when she should be dead."

Response...? Uh? How about the one I'd used in interviews when asked how I'd mustered the courage? "I was just doing my job."

"Sure. Aren't we all?"

Fuck it. If this guy wanted me dead, I had a strong feeling he would've shot me already without a word. "Is there something I can do for you, mister...?"

"I know you're working for her. Don't bother trying to deny it." He lowered the gun and moved to the seat across from me. "I want your contact."

"Contact?"

[DavidMartin: You.]

My new friend rolled his eyes and leaned closer. "Yeah, asshole. The person who hires you for jobs and pays you."

Our tram stopped and the doors opened. Twelve people filed into the train. None approached us or made eye contact with Zombie Guy. I'd keep track of them anyway. A couple sat one seat away from me.

[JSModule: How exciting. Give him this 'link code.]

[DavidMartin: Are you nuts?]

[JSModule: I'm a fan of peanuts and almonds, but not any other kinds. Give it to him.]

Fine. If he wanted me to pass that on, I'd pass it on. "Oh. I'm new to this stuff. I don't know all the lingo. His name is Mr. Smith." I recited the 'link code for him.

Zombie Guy grinned again. This time, though, I felt included in the joke. "Let me give you a quick tip, Dave." He leaned closer and lowered his voice. "Never let a guy like me get this close to you."

The gun barrel pressed against my gut.

I hadn't dealt with actual danger in a long time. At the time of my firing, my job had involved presenting a visible threat to deter problems in the first place. I was good at that.

Six years ago, I was good at this stuff.

Back then, in a situation like this, I could have kept him from firing the gun at anyone, taken it from him, and beat him enough to secure my escape.

Probably.

Assuming I took him by surprise.

On this day, holding my three-month-old son and with my skills rusty from years of disuse, I did the best I could manage. I jerked my body to one side, slapped the gun to the other, and hoped like hell no one got hurt.

The gun fired. All sound stopped. Zombie Guy's eyes widened in surprise. People panicked. I lurched to my feet. My side burned. Aaron clung to me. He probably screamed, but I couldn't hear anything.

As Zombie Guy tried to stand and point his gun at me again, the tram shuddered to a halt. We both stumbled. He fired again. Hands kept me on my feet. I kicked at Zombie Guy's gun, sending his arm upward. The gun fired for the third time.

Without a baby in my arms, I could've wrestled with him. With Aaron clutching my side for dear life, I could only kick with one foot.

People surged, carrying me away from Zombie Guy. We flooded through the open tram door in a clump.

Any moment, cops would show up. They'd swarm the area within half a minute.

I turned my back on the scene and bolted.

[DavidMartin: I need someplace to go.]

[JSModule: How fucked are you?]

[DavidMartin: I'm not sure.]

While I waited for a response, I ducked down an alley and hid behind a dumpster to catch my breath. My ears rang, which I figured was better than nothing.

[JSModule: Wake the fuck up, Dave. Did you kill him? Is there blood visible on your clothes? Is he following you? C'mon. You know how to do this. How fucked are you?]

Yes, I did know how to do this.

I checked what I could of Aaron. He seemed terrified but unharmed. As I inspected his feet, I noticed blood. This led to me noticing the ragged, bloody hole in my suit jacket.

My side blazed with pain all of a sudden.

Thinking past the agony, I assessed the situation for how hard the cops would try to find me, and whether I could walk on the street without concern or not.

[DavidMartin: I'm hit but I think it's minor, probably a graze. Dark suit plus baby means I can hide it. Can't hear anything. I only kicked the guy twice. Didn't touch the gun. Baby is crying.]

[JSModule: Much better answer. Send me your location. One of my people will arrive shortly. Do what she says.]

[DavidMartin: Yessir.]

I breathed and held the baby. The pain in my side faded enough to keep me from joining him in bawling. My hearing returned enough to let me know Aaron's cries had turned desperate and wheezy.

The woman with the belly bump and purse from the tram stepped into view.

How had I fucked up on the tram so badly? That one guy on the first job hadn't had anything competing with him for my attention. Any moron would've picked up on him. In the tram, though, I'd had two choices for who to peg as a bad actor, and I'd gotten it backward.

On the bright side, at least I'd pegged which of them wanted to take the baby. The other guy had only wanted to kill me.

[JSModule: Your contact has arrived. Her name is Carbon Shepherd.]

Carbon Shepherd almost sounded like a real name. She smiled at me.

"David or Dave?" she asked as she offered me a hand.

"Dave." I took her help because I needed it. Even with her unexpected strength pulling me to my feet, I still had to lean against the wall. The world spun a bit. "Should I call you Carbon?"

"Or Shepherd. Either way." She gestured for me to move Aaron. "Let's see the problem."

Aaron resisted as I switched him to my good side. I didn't blame him for wanting to cling to Daddy. He'd stopped screaming, at least. As soon as he discovered my other shoulder, he let me move him there.

Carbon lifted my jacket and shirt out of the way.

Ow. Ow. Fuck. Ow.

I gritted my teeth and tried not to squirm while she prodded my side.

"Bullet took a good chunk of meat. It's bleeding like hell, but you'll be fine. You'll get a scar." She pulled a small spray bottle from her purse.

"Oh good. My wife will love that."

The neon pink spray blasted my side with frigid cold. All pain from there stopped. I noticed other aches, probably bruises from the scuffle. My legs complained about all the running too.

"Chicks dig scars." Carbon put away her magic spray bottle and pulled out a wet wipe in a paper wrapper.

"What the fuck did you spray me with? Where do I get some?"

She chuckled and cleaned blood off my skin. "It's called BooBoo Goo. Antiseptic plus anesthetic with a blood-clotting agent and liquid bandage, all in one convenient spray. There's a doc in the Darkside who makes and sells it. Doc Soo. He's pretty much the only place to go if you need medical help without an implant scan."

"Good to know."

"He'll set you up right if you go down there. For a price, of course."

Of course.

Helpful advice from someone named Carbon seemed like a thing I shouldn't expect to get often. Much like gifts from Jay. "Thanks."

"You'll be fine." She wadded the wet wipe and stuffed it into her purse. "One more tip. Don't leave your blood anywhere if you can help it. Especially if you did anything even slightly illegal. The drones will pick it up. I'll dispose of this properly."

I checked my clothes. "The suit is fucked."

Carbon shrugged. "Clean up the blood and your pants will be fine. The shirt and jacket, though, yes." She reached for Aaron because obviously Jay had hired her as my babysitter.

Aaron looked at her incoming hands and shrieked. He

buried his face against my neck and shivered.

I met Carbon's somewhat bemused gaze as she withdrew. "I guess that was all a little too traumatic for him to go with a stranger right now."

"Looks like it."

The whole episode had traumatized me too. "Next time, I'll follow Jay's people."

She smirked. "Good plan. In your defense, I didn't check in because I wasn't there yet. I had no idea if it was you or not. Since I'm not babysitting, I'll tail you and act as your backup."

I knew Carbon could walk away if she wanted. Aaron had rejected her, and she'd more than covered any price Jay had agreed to pay for her services. From my perspective, anyway.

Keeping me from bleeding to death put her pretty high on my list of people to trust.

"Thanks. I appreciate that."

A notification flashed in my visual display from the Seattle Police. I stopped breathing.

"Dave? You okay?" Carbon reached for my face, peering at my eyes as she did so. "You're not falling into shock are you?"

Yes. I gulped. "I just got a message from the cops."

She shrugged like that happened to her all the time. "So open it."

"But it's from the cops."

Carbon rolled her eyes. "You were present at the scene of a crime. Just say you didn't see anything and you're not injured."

Sure, Dave, it's no big deal. Never mind the extremely illegal cable in your pocket.

I took a deep breath and opened the message.

[SeattlePD: Records indicate that you were present at the scene of a crime occurring inside a King County Metro tram on route 15 approximately ten minutes ago. An officer has been dispatched to your location to collect your statement.]

"Fuck. An officer has been dispatched to my location to collect my statement? How is that fine?"

CHAPTER 6

My savior sighed. "They're aggressive fucks today. Here, let's fix you up." She helped me tuck in my shirt and arrange the baby over the blood. "The important thing is to be clear that you didn't see anything and you're not injured. Lucky you have a baby, because you can blame things on him."

"Greetings, citizens."

Over Carbon's shoulder, I saw two cops in full uniform, complete with green and white body armor and taser batons hanging from their belts on the right side. They wore their helmets with the white face shields down.

Two cop robots entered the alley.

It sounded like the start of a joke, except I found nothing about it funny.

"Is one of you David Martin?" a synthesized cop voice asked.

Fuck. I tried with every fiber of my being not to show how little I wanted to talk to cops. My hand would not touch the pouch in my pocket with the illegal cable.

"Yes, officer, that's me."

I knew better than to shoot a message to Jay, through either of his accounts, while talking to cops in person. Even if they couldn't do half the things cops did on the shows to catch criminals, I refused to take the chance. But I thought about it. I thought about it really hard.

"And you are?" the cop asked Carbon.

She held up both hands. "A random passerby. I heard the baby crying."

"Thank you for your diligence, citizen," the other cop said to Carbon. "Please move along."

These two men sounded the same, hulked over me the same, looked the same, and acted the same. Robots with fleshy human inner bits.

Only one thing stood out as different between them. They had small numbers on their upper right chests where a name badge might go. Each had a different six-digit number displayed in green.

"Yes, sir." Carbon flashed us all a polite smile and evacuated the alley.

I hoped like hell she stayed nearby.

"Can you explain your presence on the number fifteen tram, Mr. Martin?" Cop 873217 asked.

So long as I didn't have to lie much, I thought I'd be okay. "I was going to see my wife for lunch."

Their blank faceplates stared at me.

Did I need to explain that? Maybe? "She works. I take care of the baby."

"In a suit?" Cop 623981 asked.

I felt judged. Hard. "It was either this or sweatpants. I didn't want to embarrass her."

Stop looking at my clothes. Stop looking at my clothes. Stop looking at my clothes.

"Never mind that," Cop 873217 said. Thank fuck. "Did you witness the incident on the tram?"

"No, sir." As instructed by Carbon, I used the baby. Aaron played along by hiding his face from the scary cops. "I heard a loud noise, and my son here panicked, so I got off the tram as soon as possible and ran for someplace to help him calm down."

When they said nothing, I thought maybe neither cop had ever seen a baby before. "He's only three months old," I continued, "and is pretty much my entire life right now. I don't notice a whole lot outside of him. That's why I take the tram instead of walking. So I don't walk into things."

The two cops stared at me for another few moments.

"Thank you for your cooperation, Mr. Martin," Cop 873217 said. "Your son seems calm now. Should you recall any further details regarding the incident, contact the Seattle Police as soon as possible. Please proceed on your way."

Beep boop beep.

The Seattle Police department swore up, down, sideways, and inside out that they had no robots on the streets. I totally believed them. Not.

"Yes, officer. Thank you." I tried not to hurry as I left the alley, knowing they watched me.

If they wanted to, the cops could scrutinize my message records. They'd find my brief interactions with Jay. Those messages should give the impression of someone doing odd jobs, which should seem reasonable for a guy unable to find work after a sudden firing.

Key word there—*should*.

Thank fuck I'd had the brains to send that gunman message through JSModule.

Anything else the cops found suspicious, they'd probably take to Jay instead of me. I felt confident he knew how to deal with that kind of scrutiny.

But holy shit did I shake as soon as I turned that corner. Head to toe, I thought I might shiver into pieces. Aaron curled a fist around my lapel and stuck to my shoulder like a piece of fucking fly tape.

As much as I wanted to shift the kid to my other arm, I knew I needed him to hide the blood.

I hurried down the street. At no point on my way to Lisa's work did I see Carbon. Maybe Jay had called her off.

But I had bigger problems. Me showing up with the baby would piss off Lisa. She'd demanded a babysitter. To explain, I'd have to tell her about the gunman, and I suspected she might get more angry about that.

Whether my injury would help ease her anger or not, I had no idea. Probably not?

[JSModule: What's your status?]

[DavidMartin: Two cops questioned and released me. I'm on my way to the meetup. Two blocks away.]

[JSModule: Carbon is on overwatch. Don't look for her, just trust that she's there.]

Her, I actually did trust.

Jay or his asshole friend, on the other hand, I did not.

Speaking of not trusting Jay, with my terror abated and some healthy exercise getting my blood moving in a more practical way, I had some questions for Jay. One question, really. One vitally important question.

Vital to me, anyway.

[DavidMartin: How in the fuck did that guy finger me to get to you?]

[JSModule: I'd like to know that myself.]

Somehow, I'd gotten the impression Jay knew everything that mattered. Apparently not.

[DavidMartin: He blamed me for Ms. Godhand not being dead.]

[JSModule: Did he? That's interesting. I wish you'd mentioned that sooner.]

I glared at the nearest wall as I passed it. Fuck Jay. Seriously, just fuck him.

[DavidMartin: Excuse me for not relating every tiny detail while a guy is holding a gun on me and my son. Or while I'm talking to the cops. Or, hey, maybe I should've done that while I was bleeding to death.]

[JSModule: You're kind of cranky when you get shot, Dave. Are you at the target location yet?]

Fine, Jay. Change the subject.

Lisa's glassy office building loomed ahead. Her firm occupied the tenth and eleventh floors.

[DaveMartin: I've reached the building and am heading inside.]

[JSModule: Proceed to connect with your wife. Check in as soon as you take possession of the data chip.]

Though he didn't include it in the message, I assumed he wanted me to shut the fuck up until then. His return to an automated feel for the message contents clued me in.

If he had no answer for my question, I had nothing else to say to him anyway.

Standard office building brown and beige dominated the small, carpeted lobby with its fake plants. Instead of a business pinging me when I entered, the property did. It offered me the AR directory to browse, which I used to activate one of the four elevators.

On the tenth floor, my wife sat at the receptionist desk. The wall of the faux wood desk obscured all of her below the neck. She looked up from her perch with her plastic, customer service smile. For a brief moment, she brightened, then she frowned.

I passed through a set of glass doors between the elevators and her desk to reach her. "Hi, honey, sorry I'm late. Are you ready for lunch?"

She turned her attention to the desk, which meant she looked down. "I thought you were going to get a babysitter."

"Aaron refused to go with a stranger." I smiled like I expected venomous snakes to fly out of her mouth and bite me in the face if I showed anything negative.

Lisa heaved a sigh. "Fine. Just a minute. I need to get my lunch relief. Did you get us a reservation?"

Reservation? For what? Did she think we needed to use code words for something? "Was I supposed to?"

My wife looked up at me again. She fixed me with an annoyed stare. "Did you think we could just walk into a place to eat around here at lunchtime?"

Yes, I did. "I'm sure we can find something."

"Not likely."

Another woman emerged from the depths of the architecture firm and told Lisa to go have lunch.

The elevator appeared before I opened the glass door for Lisa. She'd summoned it before I'd thought to do it.

Lunch promised a lengthy discussion of all the ways in which Dave had fucked up today. Wonderful. I could hardly wait.

We stepped into the elevator. The doors closed.

"What's the real reason we don't have a babysitter?" She stood with her arms crossed, facing the doors. Her reflection in the metal surface glared at me.

I gulped and half-wished I could face another police questioning instead. "There was an incident on the tram. Aaron got scared and wouldn't let me hand him off."

"An incident."

I waffled about how much to tell her. Of course, I couldn't really hide anything. Later tonight, she'd see the hole and blood on my shirt and jacket. Even if she missed it, the crap on my side blared neon pink.

Hiding a serious wound from my wife sounded impossible. Also stupid.

"A guy tried to kill me."

The elevator doors opened as Lisa shrieked, "What?"

Thank fuck the lobby was empty.

Aaron whimpered and leaned toward her. Lisa took the boy and stuck her hand into my pocket.

Under other circumstances, I liked having her hand in my pocket. She usually did it to inconspicuously grab my dick. This time, she only left her hand there for a moment, then she stepped out of the elevator like she meant to leave me behind forever.

Patting my pocket, I discovered a small lump I hadn't brought with me. She'd passed me the chip like a professional spy or something.

Scrambling to follow her, I tried to arrange the stupid baby bag to block the bloody hole in my suit. It rubbed against my side. Fortunately, the anesthetic still worked.

"Why did someone try to kill you? What did you do to them?" She turned to open the door with her back.

"Thanks for the vote of confidence," I grumbled.

[DavidMartin: Chip acquired.]

[JSModule: As soon as you're able, pass it to Carbon.]

[DavidMartin: Understood.]

"You aren't giving me much reason to have confidence." Lisa power-walked up the street, weaving through a scattering of pedestrians.

I had to half-jog to keep up with her. "Lisa, slow down."

She lifted her nose in the air and moved faster.

Sharp pains shot outward from the injury on my side. My body decided I needed a lot more air. Gasping for breath, I slowed to a more sedate walk and watched her bustle farther out of my reach.

Carbon stepped out of a shop as I passed and fell into

step beside me. "She looks pissed."

"She is." I retrieved the chip and handed it to her.

"Good luck, Dave. See you next time."

"Yeah."

[DavidMartin: Carbon has the chip.]

[JSModule: Carbon has already reported this. Your mission is complete. Catch the next route 15 tram to collect your payment.]

[DavidMartin: I thought you said I'd have time for lunch with my wife. I can't just walk away from her right now.]

[JSModule: Plans change when things go pear-shaped. Your wife should learn that too.]

Sure, asshole. How about you tell her?

Ahead, Lisa turned a corner. I lost sight of her. To catch the tram, I had to turn in the opposite direction.

Fuck my life.

CHAPTER 7

I opted for the money. Lisa already wanted me to go to hell. Doing something else shitty made no difference.

Clouds streaked in and dumped rain before I reached the tram stop. People crowded the plastic shelter. I waited in a downpour.

Jay was not among us. I knew I had to meet with him personally. Before he left, I needed a place I could use the cable. Why he chose not to meet me with his car, I doubted I'd ever know.

Maybe someday, he'd trust me with one of the tubes so I could use it in the safety of my own home.

Lisa chose not to message me before the tram arrived. I shuffled into the car with everyone else. It pinged my implant. Since Jay hadn't told me otherwise, I selected the stop nearest to Lisa's building. That would keep me on the tram for a while. As a bonus, I'd wind up where I could take Aaron to get him home after this fiasco.

[DavidMartin: On the tram.]

[JSModule: No shit. Behind you.]

Fuck me, I needed to work on paying attention. My job had dulled me. Years of standing watch in places where trouble rarely showed up had taken its toll.

I turned and didn't recognize the back of his head. He

held a transfer tube over his shoulder, though.

[DavidMartin: how am I supposed to use that here?]

[JSModule: The train is packed. Hold it up to your ear and keep your hand over it until you're done. Trams don't have cameras. Which is why the cops don't know you were actually involved in that business earlier.]

Taking the tube, I decided to believe him. He hadn't yet steered me wrong about this stuff. The transfer took half a minute. I held my hand over my ear while I used the cable, then palmed the cable when it finished.

As Jay had passed the tube to me, I passed it back to him.

[JSModule: You are now at the point where you can give up and turn back, Dave. Nothing you've done or seen is a big problem. Promise to keep your mouth shut, pass me the bag with the cable in it, and walk away. I trust you enough to allow that. Or keep working for me. You're rough around the edges, but I'm pretty sure you'll be fine once you get into the swing of this.]

We needed the money. Did we need it more than I needed to avoid getting shot again? I wanted to believe my life counted for more than that.

I knew better.

[DavidMartin: Do you promise you'll never involve my wife again?]

[JSModule: No. If I need plans from her firm again, I'll definitely ask for them. Other than that, though, I won't involve her on purpose. And any further requests for her help will go through you.]

Asshole knew he'd pissed me off by going to her behind my back. I supposed that counted for something.

Maybe I could find a shitty legal job someplace, but I doubted my situation would change much anytime soon.

Though I felt like I needed to talk this over with Lisa,

she and I had other things to discuss. For once in my life, I made a fucking decision. All by myself.

[DavidMartin: Then I'm good to keep working for you.]

[JSModule: Glad to hear it. Welcome to the team, Dave. I recommend visiting an implant hacker named Splice in the Darkside to shut off your GPS tracker, among other things. I can give you the initial contact. Setting up an appointment and paying for it is your problem.]

[DavidMartin: Understood. Yes, please, I'd like that contact.]

[JSModule: The guy sitting behind you is Foxtrot. He's one of my best contractors. You've met Carbon. Your job is to be able to cover for her before her pregnancy interferes too much.]

I turned again. Lo and behold, I discovered Jay's pet asshole. He grinned and let me see his profile.

"Don't get shot again," Foxtrot muttered.

"And follow you out the door next time," I said.

He grunted and returned to ignoring me.

[DavidMartin: Understood. Ping me when you need me.]

The tram informed me it had reached my stop. I joined the flow of people exiting the tram alongside the people entering it. Two blocks up, Lisa's building awaited. Still carrying that damned diaper bag, I trudged onward.

At least the downpour had faded to a light mist.

As I walked among a crowd of strangers, I realized waiting for Lisa to ping me was childish.

[DavidMartin: I lost you.]

[LisaMartin: You didn't try very hard.]

Not for the first time, I was thankful for the lack of tone in text messages.

[DavidMartin: I'm sorry.]

I pushed open the door and waited inside the lobby.

Lisa sent me nothing.

[DavidMartin: I went back to your office building.]

[LisaMartin: I'll be back there soon.]

One way or another, we'd figure out things. We always did. Maybe she'd yell at me for a while. I'd let her. A good venting session always led to great sex that night.

While waiting, I paced across the lobby, thinking about how to explain what had happened earlier. She hadn't given me a chance. Not a real one. Sure, I could've texted her, but it seemed wrong.

Like breaking up with a girlfriend by text and blocking her code instead of saying it to her face and walking away. People did that, of course. I considered it crass.

She opened the door with her face grim. "Go home," she said as she passed me the baby.

"We should talk," I said.

"Later." She shook her head and kissed Aaron's cheek. No kiss for me, of course. "I fed him."

The elevator dinged and the door opened.

"That's great, but this is important."

"It can wait." She breezed into the elevator.

I blinked at her. "Lisa, I—"

"It can wait," she growled.

The doors slid shut. I felt like she'd cut me out of something.

[DavidMartin: Lisa, I just want to explain a few things.]

[LisaMartin: I have to get back to work.]

[DavidMartin: Fine. I'll see you at home.]

I stewed. On the way to the tram, I imagined her throwing down some kind of gauntlet. Then I'd show her the neon pink holding me together. She'd fawn over it and tell me I should've said something. We'd fuck. Things would turn out okay.

Except that idea rang hollow.

For some reason, I got the feeling she wanted to divorce me. The only thing keeping us together anymore might turn out to be her desperate need for a babysitter.

Fuck me, one afternoon had exposed a lot of shit. Everything had seemed perfectly fine to me. Other than our money stress, I'd thought we had a pretty good marriage. Ten years with her had kept me on an even keel.

We never should've had a baby. The cute little boy in my arms had ruined everything.

I stepped onto a tram and thought about how to fix this.

Despite the crap, Jay's job had given us a payday almost four weeks before our next rent payment. As long as I got another call from him by then, I could afford to get her something nice.

Maybe I could pick up some real food for her. They had that at Pike Place Market. She liked real fish. For our honeymoon, instead of going someplace, we'd splurged on a fancy restaurant dinner of real food, and she'd had fresh salmon. And loved it.

My meal had passed with much less gusto. The dessert had knocked me on the floor, though. That cheesecake made from real cow's milk and eggs with a topping made from real strawberries still made my mouth water.

Aaron fell asleep on my shoulder, giving me some freedom so long as the anesthetic kept working. I spent half an hour checking booths in the enormous building to find the best deals I could on real food.

Not that I had the first fucking clue how to prepare salmon. Or any other kind of fish, for that matter. Once I found the fishmongers, I realized that inconvenient fact.

I could cook easy, forgiving things. Fish did not qualify.

"Fancy meeting you here." Carbon fell into step beside me. "And still with that bag."

To my credit, I only jumped a little.

Aaron murmured a sleepy protest.

"They give them out for free at the hospital," I said. "To hold all your baby product samples."

"Practical." She pointed at a booth with ice cream.

Beside it, a guy offered cheesecake by the slice. Yes, please. "Come here often?"

"No. I followed you."

Oh good. Someone whose job Jay wanted me to take had followed me off the clock. What could possibly go wrong?

She glanced at me like I should be offended or something. "It was easy to keep track of that bag, and you didn't try very hard."

I raised my brow. "I didn't try at all."

Carbon rolled her eyes. "Are you stupid? Do you want to get killed?"

"No?" I noticed a dull ache creeping into my side. Soon, I needed to apply some painkillers.

"Someone tried to kill you today, Dave. Does that not concern you a tiny bit?"

Not until she said something.

Carbon stopped at the ice cream booth. I kept going to the cheesecake guy. Two slices with a side of strawberry sauce seemed like a good present to help my wife lose her angry edge. He put it all into a plastic box inside a plastic bag for me.

When I rejoined Carbon, she had black-studded green ice cream in a plastic cup with a swirl of whipped cream and two bright red cherries on top.

"I can eat whatever I want," she said.

Lisa had said things like that with the exact same tone. Guilty pleasures caused guilt and pleasure.

As with my wife, I chose the path of keeping my balls intact.

"Yes, you can." And then I changed the subject. Also for self-preservation purposes. "I thought that guy was after Jay and only tried to kill me because he could."

Carbon shrugged. The line of her neck and shoulders gave me some new things to fantasize about. Before, when she'd sprayed me with that goo, I hadn't noticed the way her curves spoke of silk and steel at the same time.

"That guy was a pro," she said. "He didn't try to kill you because he could. He did it for a reason. A real reason."

I had no clue where to run with that. "Such as? He was pissed about Ms. Godhand walking after that incident with Mr. Lynch. I don't see what that has to do with me." I held up a hand to stop her from responding because that pile of shit sounded stupid even to me. "That's not what I mean. Obviously, it has something to do with me, but I'm just a security guard. He was sure I work for Jay and sounded like he didn't give a fuck about me. Maybe he did it because he thought it would sting Jay or Ms. Godhand."

She licked her spoon in a way that made me wish I could ask her for a blow job. "Maybe. More likely he considered you a witness to eliminate. Or he's personally pissed you stopped that cop from shooting her. In which case, that's kind of interesting, isn't it?"

"Sure, but not to me." I shrugged. "I like Ms. Godhand. She was a good boss. But she's a rich, powerful lady. I'll bet plenty of people were disappointed she didn't die that day."

"Are you ready to die for her?" She tossed the question like it meant nothing more than a casual, anonymous fuck.

I snorted and thought about running my hands over her ass. That casual, anonymous fuck sounded pretty good. "No."

She slapped me across the face. That hand moved so fast I never saw it coming. My cheek stung and my dick twitched.

If I could have, I would've bent her over right there.

"If you're not paying attention," she whispered into my ear, "you might." Her breath puffed down my neck. "I could gut you right now."

"I'd rather you fuck me."

She laughed and smacked me in the ass. "Be careful what you wish for, Dave." With a dark grin, she walked away from me. Her ass swished back and forth. She beckoned for me to follow her with a swish of two fingers.

I'd like to say that I turned around and went straight home, secure in the knowledge that my wife and I would patch things up and not throw away ten years together. That the baby on my arm reminded me of Lisa enough to stop me. We had a three-month-old son. She had a good job with insurance. Our marriage had weathered a lot already. Before Aaron, we'd enjoyed a good sex life.

As I watched Carbon's curves, I couldn't remember any of that. I saw Lisa's anger. That growl in her words, promising a shouting match later, lingered in my head. Then I thought about how easily she'd abandoned me for Aaron, over and over. After him, our sex life had become a chain of teasing starts with no finishes.

I never would have sought out Carbon or anyone else. This willing, wanton woman felt like a slice of cheesecake sitting out, waiting for me. If I didn't eat it, someone else would. And then I'd get nothing.

Fuck that.

CHAPTER 8

Two hours later, I stood in our small shower while Aaron slept in our bed. The warm water blasted my face and streamed down my body. My side ached through the painkillers Carbon had offered. Thin streaks of neon pink ran down my leg to swirl with the water as it sluiced into the drain.

Carbon had said the wound crap dissolved in water, so either avoid long showers for the next week or go get my own damned can of goo. As soon as I had enough extra money to afford it, I had a date in the Darkside with an implant hacker and a doctor. Their prices ran steep.

I needed more work. Carbon had suggested going to see them and asking if they needed anything done as payment. Until I had some more experience with all this illegal shit under my belt, I had to think about it.

They'd probably want things I had no knowledge of how to handle.

When I turned off the water, I wondered if I needed a separate bank account. Lisa could manage our shared finances. As long as I handed over enough to cover my part of the bills, she had nothing to complain about.

She probably wouldn't approve of the kinds of things Carbon had suggested I do to set myself up.

Carbon had explained a hell of a lot more than Jay ever would. In the business, they referred to people like me as "meat." As in meat for the grinder. We did bodyguard and lookout work. Meat took the hits so other people could get their shit done.

It sounded like a shit job. On the other hand, it paid well.

If I wanted to do this work, I'd need BooBoo Goo, a gun, a blade of some kind, personal transportation, and probably a way to lift weights. Basic tools, body armor, and medical supplies would help.

Since she hoped to get back to the work at some point after her baby, Carbon had refused to part with any of her kit. The advice and list, though, complete with ballpark prices, was plenty. I had a lot to go on and a much better idea of what to do on any given mission.

Most importantly, I knew I could never again bring Aaron to any mission. Not even for the initial part where I needed to pass him to a babysitter. If that ever had to happen in the future, I'd demand to meet that person well away from the mission zone.

Carbon had offered to try babysitting again for us. She wanted more experience with babies and liked getting paid for it. If I did that, I'd take Aaron to her place.

I'd have the pickup to look forward to after a successful mission.

When I dried myself after the shower, I decided not to wear a shirt. Lisa needed to know I'd taken a bullet. Earlier, I'd stumbled in the face of her anger.

As usual.

I found Aaron waking up and hungry, so I took him to the couch and fed him a bottle while I watched the news. Time slipped past. Nothing seemed real or important.

Lisa came home.

The moment she walked in the door and I saw her, reality slammed down on me.

I'd cheated on my wife.

Like a piece of shit, I sat on the couch with our baby sleeping in my arms. As if nothing had happened. For one hour of absolute bliss, I'd pissed on everything that mattered to me. Then I'd floated around like I hadn't betrayed my wife.

The most beautiful woman on Earth paused at the mouth of our hallway and blinked at me. "Why are you pink?"

What the fuck had I been thinking? What the fuck had I done? What the fuck did I do? "Pink?"

"On your side." She shuffled across the room, pointing.

I looked down and remembered useful things. "Oh. I got shot earlier." Why did I sound like it wasn't a big deal? Who was this asshole on the couch?

"You got shot." She blinked at me, her brow furrowed in confusion. "When did you get shot?"

"Earlier, on the tram." I shrugged.

This conversation felt like an out-of-body experience. Some strange man sat on the couch with the baby, unconcerned with anything that hadn't killed him.

"Was this the 'incident' you mentioned? Which happened before you met me to get the chip? You did say someone tried to kill you."

"Yes." The asshole on the couch shrugged again. "I tried to tell you what happened, but looking back, I think I was a little bit in shock still."

She kept staring at me like I'd sprouted antlers or something.

In fairness to her, I felt the same.

Part of me needed to tell her about Carbon. I'd done something horrible and deserved whatever she wanted to do to me.

The rest of me sat on the couch, talking to her. That guy sounded like he'd taken Aaron for a walk and nothing terribly stressful had happened. The dalliance with Carbon hadn't meant anything to him. He'd blown off some steam and eased some stress. Like getting a massage.

This was maybe what going insane felt like.

She opened her mouth and shut it without saying anything.

I waited.

"Is it bad?" She took a step closer to me.

If I wanted to, I could take her hand and pull her onto the couch. "I'm drugged up for the pain. Not serious, though."

"Oh, you're on painkillers. No wonder you seem so dopey." She sighed and picked up Aaron. "Maybe we should order out for dinner."

Dinner, right. We needed to eat food. "I got some cheesecake."

She frowned at me as she shifted to take Aaron to the bedroom. "Why?"

"You were upset."

With a roll of her eyes, she stalked out of the room. "Honestly, Dave, you can be such an idiot."

What did that have to do with anything? "Do you want me to order something?"

"No, you'll mess it up."

Why did I feel guilty about Carbon again?

Right. Because I loved my wife. Something something richer and poorer, good times and bad.

I rubbed my face and tried to stop thinking about her body. Carbon had tough skin, thick muscle, and a variety of battle and surgical scars. She'd done the meat job for five years already. Some of her survival abilities came from illegal implants in various parts of her body.

Carbon had strongly recommended I invest in a few specific implants.

It's only illegal if they scan you. Like Jay had told me before, if they get to that, you're already fucked anyway.

About twenty minutes later, Lisa returned in her sweatpants and nursing bra. She'd probably given Aaron a feeding and put him down for a nap. The sight of her soft, pale skin made me want to touch her.

I thought about the things I used to do to her in bed. When had I last seen her fully naked? A month or so before the baby, I thought. When she'd gotten close to the due date, she'd started wearing the nursing bras to hold her breasts off her belly.

Sex had turned into an engineering problem. I remembered giving up on trying to solve it.

As she stepped into the kitchen, the building notified me we had a visitor.

Lisa opened the door and left to handle it. Without a shirt. Or a word.

Apparently, I'd proven myself incompetent.

A few minutes later, she returned with a plastic bag from our usual Chinese place. I stood and fetched plates and utensils. The thought crossed my mind that I should mention the shirt issue. Did it matter, though? If she wanted to walk around in her bra, I had no good reason to stop her. It showed less than some bathing suits, especially with sweatpants.

"I'm sorry," I said as she handed me a plastic box. The

rice inside smelled like chicken. What exactly did I apologize for? Too many options to decide.

She sighed and said nothing. We dumped food onto our plates and traded boxes. Hers had a pile of soy blocks in brown sauce that smelled like salty oranges. Everything a healthy adult human needs to survive, all packed into one concentrated block of pure nutrition.

We usually got food that seemed more like food when we ordered out. I preferred the Mexican place, where they made the soy smooth and cheesy inside a tortilla.

"You shouldn't spend that much on a dessert," she finally said as we sat and regarded our non-food food.

The soy blocks suddenly felt like a punishment for daring to blow money on real cheesecake.

"I just want you to be happy."

She pursed her lips like I'd offered the worst reason imaginable. "I'm putting a block on your account access so you can't spend that much without getting my permission first."

I stopped with my fork halfway to my mouth and blinked at her. "Excuse me?"

"I can't trust you to stick to our budget." She stuffed a rice-decorated block into her mouth. "If this is how you're going to act every time you get hurt, I have to keep you from doing anything dumb."

In a moment, my guilt evaporated. This woman, my wife, wanted to treat me like a child. "I can still do math, Lisa."

"You're getting paid irregularly." She shrugged like this whole thing was no big deal. "We can't rely on your income. It'll take a while to adjust to that. We need to build up some savings as a cushion. When we reach that point, I'll lift the block."

Yes, I needed a separate account. I could have Jay's payments go there, then keep half and funnel the rest into our shared account. That way I could save up for the things I needed without having to go through my accountant gatekeeper.

"Fine," I grumbled into my food.

She jerked her hand toward me like she considered touching mine but thought better of it. "It's not that I don't trust you, Dave. It's that you're acting like one extra payday means we're all set. This is just to help you adjust to the new situation. We have a baby to think about. If the bills don't get paid, we're much more screwed than before."

Baby this, baby that, baby all the things. "Everything is about the baby."

Lisa arched an eyebrow. "That's how babies are. They're demanding and time-consuming. You know that. It doesn't last forever."

Sure. No problem. Just give up everything to the baby for three or four years. Carry on. Nothing to see here.

I loved my son, but damn, did he need a lot of maintenance and attention.

Instead of answering, I shoved more food into my mouth. We never should've had a baby.

"Maybe you need to get out more."

Maybe I needed to have a drink and fuck my wife.

Or maybe I needed to have a drink and fuck Carbon again.

Lisa pushed food around her plate. "You were happier when you pretended to still have your job. It could be because of the fresh air and exercise. You could try taking a walk in the evening when Jay doesn't need you."

Sure. Fresh air. Exercise. Or, you know, bald-faced lying to your face, dear.

If she wanted me to put on a fake smile, I could put on a fake smile. "I'm sorry I'm grumpy. It's been a long time since I got hurt on the job." Look at your happy monkey, dancing for you.

Her mouth twitched into a faint smile. "I remember when you broke your arm that one time. You were miserable and grumpy then too."

"Yeah." Pain did that to people. Murder attempts did too. So did guilt, but I wasn't so sure I had a whole lot of that.

The baby screeched. Lisa left. I got up to do the dishes.

A notification popped into my vision for a message from the Seattle Police.

Fuck.

CHAPTER 9

Like I had earlier in the day, I stared at the message and thought about how many horrible things it might contain. I heard an echo of Carbon's voice telling me to deal with it and open the message.

[SeattlePolice: Your presence is required in the lobby of your building. Please proceed to that location as soon as possible.]

Fuck.

I'd put the illegal cable on the dresser in the bedroom. Nothing else about my person should show as illicit in a scan. Until I got some of those modifications I wanted, I could talk to cops without worrying about the scan problem.

Carbon had eased my fears on that front quite a bit.

Drying my hands on a towel, I hurried to the bedroom for a shirt. They might ask about the pink stuff, but only if they could see it. If I could avoid lying about anything, I wanted to.

"The cops want to see me in the lobby. It's probably about that thing on the tram."

Lisa sat with Aaron, holding him against her chest and rocking back and forth. "Don't screw it up."

Yet another vote of confidence from my loving wife. "Thanks." I snagged a shirt and pulled it on as I left the room.

I heard her sigh behind me.

Fuck me, we had to fix this shit between us. I had no idea how, but it had to happen.

She didn't need to know about Carbon. Ever. I could look at that as a one-time thing. Lisa wouldn't gripe about me getting a professional massage, except for the price. If someone wanted to give me one for free, no problem.

This massage had escalated beyond professional, of course. I didn't have to tell her about it.

Sure. It would only eat at me from the inside for the rest of my life.

Fuck me. I had to tell her. Not today, but I had to say something. She deserved so much better from me. Maybe I could spin it as a drug-induced lapse of judgment caused by sexual frustration.

And also, maybe I could hope she decided to castrate me instead of cutting off my dick.

Enough about this, though.

Walking down the hall, I had a thought to wonder why the cops wanted to see me in the lobby. They had access to get to any floor they wanted in any building at any time.

The elevator doors opened for me. An unfamiliar guy in a suit about the same as either of mine nodded to me as he stepped out and I stepped in. I thought I'd at least seen all our neighbors.

"Hey," I said, holding the door open and leaning out to get a better look at him.

The guy raised a hand without turning as he headed toward our end. "Hey."

"Are you new to the building?"

"Yep." He glanced over his shoulder. "Sorry, I'm in a hurry. We can meet and greet later."

"Sure." I let go of the door.

The elevator closed. I crossed my arms and waited while it carried me downstairs. One of our neighbors had moved out and someone else had moved in without me noticing.

We had a baby, after all. Everything else took second place. All the time. No matter what.

I pinched the bridge of my nose and tried not to think about anything in particular. At least I knew we wouldn't have a second kid. Not with how much the first stressed us.

Not if I kept thinking about Carbon and her tongue. She had great fingers too. Hot damn, that ass.

The elevator reached the ground floor and the doors opened. A blur of gray and denim rushed into the elevator. Something hit me in the side where I'd taken the bullet. Sharp, severe pain made me cry out.

I doubled over. Old, rusty instinct and faded muscle memory sent me lurching at my attacker.

My shoulder hit his gut. We slammed into the opposite wall. He grunted. So did I.

Adrenaline flooded my entire being. Though I hadn't done this in a long time, I still knew what to do. My body remembered how to handle the rush and what it meant.

I clamped my hands onto his shoulder and forced him into my knee.

He held a pistol. Wheezing and gasping, he tried to turn it toward me. I chopped at his arm. He dropped the gun.

I recognized the zombie guy from the tram. What the fuck?

This time, with no baby to worry about, I beat the shit out of him. He moved like he had serious training, but he'd probably expected that first blow to take me down.

Once again, my reaction had taken him by surprise. That shoulder to his gut had given me enough of an advantage to put him on the ground. Even with the injury and painkillers in my system.

Later, when the rush wore off, I'd curl into a ball and hate life for whatever fresh damage he'd caused to my side.

For the moment, I picked up the gun and pointed it at him. He lay on the floor with his feet preventing the elevator door from closing.

"What the fuck do you want from me, asshole? I already told you my contact." I checked the chamber and found a round ready and waiting. Years ago, I'd known a lot of different guns on sight. This one, I couldn't remember the manufacturer or model name, but I knew it used bullets without cartridges and had baffles inside to muffle the noise. If he'd used it on the tram, I wouldn't have lost my hearing.

That gun, I hadn't gotten a good look at because of Aaron. I suspected he'd brought a cheaper one onto the tram because he'd intended to discard it after killing me.

This gun, he would keep.

He expected to get away with killing me in my apartment building.

The guy laughed between labored breaths. "You're one of her people."

Her people. Victoria Godhand. "So what?"

"So that makes you the enemy, moron."

Enemy. He considered me his enemy. Yet one more person thought I needed punishment for doing my fucking job. As if getting fired and blacklisted from honest work across Seattle hadn't done enough to me and my family.

I stomped on his balls. Laugh that off, asshole.

Checking behind me, I confirmed the cops had not actually arrived. Of course they hadn't. I should've noticed the fake ID stamp. The cops used "SeattlePD" to message people, not "SeattlePolice."

"Cute trick with the spoofing," I snapped.

"Worked," the guy said, his voice much higher in pitch than before.

What did I do with this guy? I had no idea what us illegal types did with people who belonged in a hole, so I messaged JSModule.

[DavidMartin: That guy who tried to kill me on the tram just showed up at my apartment complex and tried to kill me again. What do I do with him?]

While waiting for a response, I had a thought to wonder about the guy in the suit. A minute or so earlier and he would've been in the lobby when this guy attacked me. This asshole had taken a hell of a chance. One witness made everything more complicated.

[JSModule: Is he dead?]

[DavidMartin: No. I beat him up and took his gun. He said I'm the enemy because I work for Ms. Godhand.]

[JSModule: In that case, kill him.]

I blinked at my prisoner. He still lay on the floor holding his privates.

[DavidMartin: Excuse me?]

[JSModule: With that tidbit, I know who he works for. He might have some useful information, but I can't get anyone there to pick him up anytime soon, which makes him a liability because you have no experience holding or interrogating prisoners. Him escaping at this point is much more problematic than him escaping earlier.]

On one hand, I appreciated Jay taking the time to compose an actual explanation. On the other hand, I had never killed another human being before and preferred not to start.

I stood at the top of a slippery slope, peering down and wondering how bad the bottom might be. Pretty bad, probably.

[DavidMartin: I'm not here to kill people for you.]

[JSModule: You're not killing him for me. You're killing him for you, your wife, and your son. If you think for one moment he hasn't already reported his failure, you're living in a fantasyland. Kill this guy to send a message that you're not to be fucked with. They should back off.]

He made too much sense. I gulped. Blood rushed in my ears.

[DavidMartin: I'm not sure there are no cameras here.] Considering the quality of the gun in my hand, I had strong suspicions, but betting my life on a suspicion sounded stupid.

[JSModule: I have a hacker who can take care of that for you. Contacting him now.]

The guy on the floor shifted his breathing. Despite his effort to fake it, I could tell he'd recovered from his distress and had thoughts about jumping me. In a mild panic, I fired the gun at his head.

As expected, the report sounded lesser than the one on the tram despite the smaller space. Instead of deafening me, it pinged my ears and made them mad for a few seconds.

Blood, bone, and brain splattered on the floor. His eyes rolled up and his body collapsed into a limp heap. The bullet had hit him in the forehead, slightly to the left.

I'd taken a life. A surprising kind of calm settled over me. Sort of the reverse of panic.

Idly, I considered that I should do some target practice. That bullet should've hit in the center.

[DavidMartin: Shit. Now I have a mess.]

A mess with a particular stench I hadn't smelled in years. The longer I stood there, the worse it grew.

In this bizarre mental state, I thought of the strange man in the suit. Yes, it had been a risk for Zombie Guy to come here and try to take me in the elevator. A big risk.

A stupid risk.

Unless he had an accomplice.

Someone who looked like he belonged in the building. For example, a man in a relatively cheap suit.

Fuck.

I kicked the corpse's feet into the elevator and punched the button for fifteen.

[JSModule: I can handle that too. Just so you know, this kind of cleanup doesn't come cheap. You can work it off, though. I know you're not exactly swimming in money.]

Great. I had my wife and kid to worry about. I could practically see their corpses already. In five minutes, the amount of time since I'd let the elevator doors close on the fifteenth floor, a professional like the dead guy on the floor could have easily broken into the apartment and murdered both Lisa and Aaron.

I'd seen enough of his face. He wouldn't escape me forever.

The cool, rational man inside my body prepared for three distinct possibilities. One, I could find two corpses. Two, I could find two hostages. Three, I could discover signs of a struggle and no one home. I also accepted the possibility I'd discover a combination. With two people involved, this suit guy had a lot of options.

Zombie Guy had called me the enemy.

Until he'd tried to kill me, I hadn't cared about him at all. Even after that, I'd only wanted him not to try to kill me again. Whoever he'd worked for could've avoided having me after him.

[DavidMartin: I would like to know who declared war on me today.]

[JSModule: Ross Lynch, CEO of Godhand International. He's at war with Victoria Godhand, not you.]

[DavidMartin: I can assure you that he is most definitely at war with me. Whether he intends it or not.]

[JSModule: I'll keep that in mind as I consider what to have you do to repay the services you're using tonight.]

[DavidMartin: You do that.]

The elevator doors opened. I jogged down the hall and tossed open the door, expecting someone to shoot through the doorway.

No gunshots. Exposing as little of myself as possible, I peered around the frame.

Empty.

I listened.

The fridge buzzed a low hum I'd long since learned to tune out. Air blew from the vents as it always did, keeping the temperature steady.

Nothing else. No breathing, no sobbing, no crying.

I knew that stench.

Fuck.

CHAPTER 10

I slipped across the room with my gun pointed up and the safety still off. Wary as fuck despite the lack of noise, I ducked my head into the hallway and pulled back before committing. At the other end of the short hallway, I did the same.

Every step took me deeper into the stench of death.

In the dim light, I saw Lisa lying on the bed. Her blood already soaked the sheets.

The cool, rational asshole inside me checked inside the room for threats. From the lack of gore spatter, he'd probably pushed her down before shooting her.

Before feeling anything, I checked everywhere for Aaron's corpse.

No sign of the baby. Also missing? His diaper bag.

Not missing? The small black bag with my induction cable. It still lay on the dresser.

By this point, the suit guy already had Aaron beyond my reach. I ran for the balcony anyway, hoping against hope to see something.

In the darkness, with my stomach churning in the sudden slap of cold, fresh air, I saw the blinking lights of a black car rising from the street. The odds of that car not holding my son were so astronomical, I almost laughed at the idea of it.

As I pinged the vehicle for its plate number, I raised my gun and fired at the car. A tiny spark skipped off the frame.

[DavidMartinSystem: Error. The vehicle you are attempting to identify does not exist.]

For good measure, I put a second and third bullet into it before the car outdistanced the gun's range.

[DavidMartin: That fucker took my son. I hit the car three times.]

Along with that, I passed on the error message.

[JSModule: That means they have a jammer. What fucker is this?]

I sent a description of the suit and how he'd gotten past me.

[DavidMartin: He killed my wife and took my son.]

With the information dispensed, I sagged under the weight of grief. I shuffled inside and returned to Lisa's cooling corpse.

[JSModule: I'm sorry. That's not right. We don't usually fuck with families. These assholes are playing a harder game than we thought.]

[DavidMartin: This is not a fucking game.]

For the last day of Lisa's life, we'd argued, I'd cheated on her and lied to her, and someone had taken her baby. Everything had gone wrong.

I should've been the one to take the bullet to the brain, not her. I'd deserved it, not her.

[JSModule: No. It's not a fucking game. It's a war. As soon as I have information about your son's whereabouts, that's your mission.]

Yes. Total agreement. No argument. If it would lead to my son, I would wade through anything.

[JSModule: At the moment, though, you have a bigger problem. Someone called the cops to your building, reporting a dead body. My people aren't going to arrive before them. You have about two minutes to get the fuck out of there and head north. Once you're clear, I'll pick you up.]

Spurred by that anti-panic again, I whirled into motion. I yanked the wedding ring off Lisa's still-warm finger, snagged the black bag with the induction cord, and grabbed a change of clothes. All those things plus the gun got stuffed into a small backpack. On my way out, for no reason I could possibly explain, I took the bag with the cheesecake.

[DavidMartin: Can you pick me up on the roof?]

[JSModule: Not close enough to get there and out in time.]

Great.

One of our elevators had a dead body. Cops would head there first. They'd check every elevator. Probably, they'd do a building-wide scanner sweep to ping every implant present.

I had to get out before they began that sweep.

Fifteen fucking flights of stairs. At least I took them down and not up. Thank fuck they acted as the fire escape, because that meant they had a separate outside access door.

Huffing and puffing, I burst outside. In the distance, I heard approaching sirens. They sounded close. Way too close.

Nothing mattered except escaping the scene. I ran. Hard. Fast. Up the street. People squawked as I shoved them aside.

Light blared over me.

"David Martin," a man's amplified voice shouted at me. The sound echoed off nearby buildings. "Stop where you are."

Like fuck would I do that.

[DavidMartin: I have a small problem.]

[JSModule: That's one way to put it. They're tracking your implant, so you need to get to a dead zone.]

[DavidMartin: I don't suppose you know of any besides the Darkside?]

[JSModule: None nearby. If you can get eyes off you, I can scoop you up and get you there. I doubt you'll make it to the Darkside on foot before they shoot you.]

People on the street dove out of my way. Thank fuck no one tried to be heroic and tackle me.

I headed in a straight line until I reached the next intersection. There, I turned the corner and headed in a different straight line.

[DavidMartin: Where are you?]

"David Martin, this is your final warning. Stop now or we will open fire."

[JSModule: Turn left. Head into the park. Use the trees for cover. I'm on the other side of the park in my usual black sedan.]

I turned left, dodged two ground vehicles, and headed into a park occupying half a city block. Trees lined the outer edge.

As soon as I hit the first tree, I spun on my heels and ran in the opposite direction. This got the spotlight off my back.

My side hurt like fuck. I tasted blood and had to gasp for breath. Every part of me wanted to lie down and let the cops kill me or taser me, or whatever they wanted to do.

Without Lisa, who I'd betrayed and disrespected on the last day of her life, I saw no real point to continuing.

For my son, I would keep going.

No matter what I said or did, the cops wouldn't believe I shot Zombie Guy in self-defense. Not with the bullet in his forehead like that. As soon as someone noticed Lisa, they'd assume I'd also killed my wife and abducted my son.

Nothing would explain my motive, but absolutely no

one in Seattle PD would give a flying fuck about that.

Fleeing the scene, as far as the cops cared, proved my guilt.

They could find Aaron by pinging his implant right up until his kidnapper brought my son into a dead zone. By Jay's answer about that of "none nearby," I knew they could take him someplace other than the Darkside.

They would.

These people would risk nothing. They'd get their own implant hacker to do whatever implant hackers did. Then the cops would assume I'd killed my own son and ditched the body in the Darkside.

After all, as far as they knew, I'd killed my wife. Why not the baby too?

Ahead, I saw Jay's car lurking in a dark space between two streetlights. He'd parked with the passenger door on my side. To reach it, I had to cross maybe twenty feet of exposed sidewalk.

The cops overhead knew where to find my implant. Their spotlight roved along my path as if it pinged a second behind me.

I kept running. My life depended on it. Aaron's life depended on it.

From somewhere deep down, I dragged the dregs of my energy to the surface.

Jay's car door popped open. I sprinted and dove inside. The door shut.

I gasped for breath.

"Hang on," Jay said as the car shot into the air.

The guy could fly a car. We rolled and turned tight corners. Under other circumstances, I probably would've yelled at him for all the lunatic maneuvers.

"We're clear," he said as he righted the car. "My jammer

is active and we have no tail, so you're safe."

That one little word undid me. The cool, rational asshole shattered and I collapsed into incoherent sobbing.

Jay said something and I didn't give a fuck.

At some point, he stopped driving and I still didn't give a fuck.

He waited. About twenty minutes later, a fact I knew thanks to the timestamp in my visual display, I wiped my face one more time on my shirt and stared out the windshield.

I felt...empty. Worse than empty. Like a black hole existed inside me.

The car sat in the parking area for an old gas station with two closed repair bays. A warm light glowed in the window around the edges of closed blinds. On the front glass door, a painted sign read Welcome.

"I'm going to rip out his fucking spine with my bare hands." I sounded like I'd gargled gravel.

"As soon as I figure out who he is, I'll arrange for that," Jay said as if he commented on the weather.

Good. He took me seriously and had no objections.

"Where are we?" I pointed at the gas station building.

Jay stared out the front windshield. "I've booked Splice, the amazing implant hacker, for you tonight. We need to get your GPS tracker shut off and set you up so you can avoid law enforcement entanglements. Splice can do that. I'll cover the cost."

"Thanks." I meant it. He could've decided to make me work for it. "Then what?"

"Then I'll stash you someplace for a little while and you'll do some training to get your shit together. We'll get you some upgrades and let you get used to them. When you're ready, you're going to work for me. And you're going to trust me that every mission you work on is at least tangentially related to finding and retrieving your son."

"A little while." He wanted me to wait. While those people did who knew what the fuck to my son, he expected me to sit and wait.

Jay shrugged and still stared out the windshield. "You're no good to me on the ragged edge. You're no good to anyone like this. Especially not Aaron."

"You're an asshole," I grumbled.

He smirked. "So are you, Dave. So are you. I'll be back in the morning. I expect you to have a fake name by then."

"Yes, sir." I stepped out of the car and shuffled toward the light. With my fucking cheesecake.

Other Books by the Author

Darkside Seattle
Street Doc
Fixer
Mechanic
Hacker
Meat
Sniper (coming soon)
Ghost (coming soon)

as Lee French
Maze Beset trilogy
superheroes in denim
Dragons In Pieces
Dragons In Chains
Dragons In Flight

Tales of Ilauris
sword & sorcery fantasy
Damsel In Distress
Shadow & Spice
Al-Kabar

The Greatest Sin series
epic snark fantasy
co-authored with Erik Kort
The Fallen
Harbinger
Moon Shades
Illusive Echoes
A Curse of Memories
Charred Roots

Anthologies
Merely This and Nothing More: Poe Goes Punk
Unnatural Dragons: a science fiction anthology
What We've Unlearned: English Class Goes Punk
Undercurrents: What Lies Beneath
Hideous Progeny: Horror Goes Punk
Enter the Aftermath
Swords, Sorcery, & Self-Rescuing Damsels
Noise: a speculative fiction anthology
Well...It's Your Cow
Taught By Time: Myth and Legend Goes Punk

co-authored with Jeffrey Cook
Superheroes
Nova Ranger Academy

Space Opera
Dragoncaller
A Foundation of Gravestones (coming soon)
The Last Armada (coming soon)

WWW.AUTHORLEEFRENCH.COM

About the Author

L.E. French is the cyberpunk pseudonym of Lee French, a *USA Today* bestselling fantasy and science fiction author. She lives in Olympia, WA with two kids, two bicycles, and too much stuff. An avid gamer, compulsive writer, and casual cyclist, she can often be found on myth-weavers.com, sitting in her Squishy Chair of Inspiration +4, or riding her bike around the city.

Best known for Spirit Knights, a young adult urban fantasy series, she is an active member of the the Science Fiction and Fantasy Writers of America and a Municipal Liaison for the NaNoWriMo Olympia region.

Thank you for reading! If you enjoyed this story, please consider posting a review wherever you buy your books.

www.ingramcontent.com/pod-product-compliance
Lightning Source LLC
Chambersburg PA
CBHW030648190726

48286CB00008B/2723